WARRIORS

WARRIOR'S RETURN

CREATED BY
ERIN HUNTER

WRITTEN BY
DAN JOLLEY

HAMBURG // LONDON // LOS ANGELES // TOKYO

HarperCollins*Publishers*

Warrior's Return
Created by Erin Hunter
Written by Dan Jolley
Art by James L. Barry

Lettering - Lucas Rivera
Cover Design - Anne Marie Horne

Editor - Lillian Diaz-Przybyl
Digital Imaging Manager - Chris Buford
Pre-Production Supervisor - Erika Terriquez
Art Director - Anne Marie Horne
Production Manager - Elisabeth Brizzi
VP of Production - Ron Klamert
Editor-in-Chief - Rob Tokar
Publisher - Mike Kiley
President and C.O.O. - John Parker
C.E.O. and Chief Creative Officer - Stuart Levy

A  Manga

TOKYOPOP Inc.
5900 Wilshire Blvd. Suite 2000
Los Angeles, CA 90036

E-mail: info@TOKYOPOP.com
Come visit us online at www.TOKYOPOP.com

For information address HarperCollins Children's Books, a division of HarperCollins Publishers, 195 Broadway, New York, NY 10007
www.harpercollinschildrens.com

Library of Congress catalog card number: 2007935238
ISBN 978-0-06-125233-4

19 20 LSC 23
❖
First Edition

Dear readers,

Did you guess what would be waiting for Graystripe
when he returned to the forest? His Clanmates gone,
the camp destroyed in a swath of logs and mud, no
sign that generations of cats had lived, hunted, and
worshipped there for countless moons . . . Far from
being the end of Graystripe and Millie's long journey,
it's only the beginning. And this time they have no idea
where they are going!

Will Graystripe and Millie make it to the sun-drown-
place and find the scattered Clans? Join them on the
final part of their adventure right to the edge of the
earth, following the sign of the dying warrior.

Sincerely,
Erin Hunter

EVERYTHING'S SMASHED... WRECKED... DESTROYED.

THE HIGHROCK...

...THE FERN TUNNEL...

...THE APPRENTICES' DEN...

...EVEN THE ELDERS' TREE.

EVERYTHING I'VE EVER KNOWN... MY WHOLE LIFE.

TORN TO PIECES.

ONLY THE MEDICINE CATS' DEN MADE IT THROUGH.

PART OF ME THINKS, MAYBE IF I GO TO SLEEP HERE, I'LL WAKE UP AND EVERYTHING WILL BE BACK TO NORMAL.

EVERYTHING WILL BE GOOD AGAIN.

HOW THEY TREATED OUR WOUNDS... HEALED THE SICK... INTERPRETED DREAMS...

SHE LISTENS CLOSELY, BUT THEN IT ALL HITS ME AGAIN. MY HOME IS GONE. DESTROYED... BY TWOLEGS.

STARCLAN FORGIVE ME... I HATE THEM SO MUCH.

IT'LL BE ALL RIGHT, GRAYSTRIPE. WE'LL GET THROUGH THIS.

YOU SHOULD TRY TO GET SOME SLEEP. OKAY?

MILLIE'S SWEET. I KNOW SHE CARES ABOUT ME.

BUT I WON'T BE SLEEPING TONIGHT.

MILLIE'S WORDS STICK IN MY HEAD AS WE GO OUT TO HUNT ONE LAST TIME.

SHE'S RIGHT. I CAN'T GIVE UP YET.

NOT ON THUNDERCLAN.

SO... WHERE TO NOW?

THAT'S A GOOD QUESTION. I'VE GOT TO FIND FIRESTAR AGAIN. HE'D NEVER STOP SEARCHING FOR ME.

BUT ALL I KNOW IS THAT SOME OF MY CLANMATES CAME BACK FROM THE SUN-DROWN-PLACE WITH A MESSAGE...

WE GO WEST.

...THAT A DYING WARRIOR WOULD SHOW THEM THE WAY TO A NEW HOME.

THAT'S THE BEST I CAN DO.

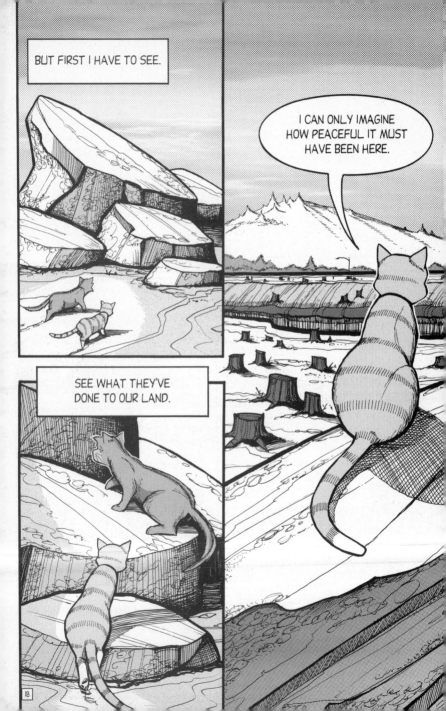

WELL... MOSTLY. YES.
WE LIVED OUR LIVES IN THIS PLACE... SOME OF THE MEMORIES HURT.
SILVERSTREAM... IT'S NOT BAD ENOUGH THAT I LOST YOU HERE.
NOW I'VE LOST EVERYTHING ELSE.

THERE.

I KNOW THAT PLACE.

MILLIE DOESN'T COMPLAIN.

WE HAVE TO SNEAK PAST THESE SLEEPING MONSTERS...FIGHT OUR WAY THROUGH THE MUD...AND SHE NEVER SAYS A WORD.

I'M LUCKY TO HAVE HER WITH ME.

THE DYING WARRIOR? WHO WAS IT?

DO YOU KNOW WHERE THEY WENT?

NOT A LIVING WARRIOR. IT WAS A SHOOTING STAR, THE LIGHT OF ONE OF OUR WARRIOR ANCESTORS FLICKERING OUT, FAR ON THE HORIZON.

TOWARD THE SETTING SUN. I WENT WITH THEM AS FAR AS HIGH-STONES, WHICH IS WHERE BRAMBLE-CLAW RECEIVED A SIGN...

SO--HOW WERE THEY? HOW DID THEY SEEM?

THIN... SCARED... BUT THEY HAD FAITH.

THEY KNEW STARCLAN WOULD LEAD THEM TO THEIR NEW HOME.

THEY ASKED ME TO GO WITH THEM.

BUT THIS IS MY HOME NOW... PLUS I KNEW I COULD SEND YOU THEIR WAY, IF I EVER SAW YOU.

HOW LONG AGO WAS THIS? WHEN YOU SAW THEM?

OH... THAT WAS... SEASONS AGO. MANY SEASONS AGO.

THEY WERE ALIVE WHEN RAVENPAW SAW THEM, BUT SO MUCH TIME HAS PASSED...!

THEY COULD HAVE BEEN BROKEN UP BY DISASTERS... OR JUST SCATTERED... OR FOUGHT AMONG THEMSELVES AGAIN.

IT BARELY EVEN REGISTERS WHEN RAVENPAW ASKS US IF WE WANT TO STAY THE NIGHT IN THE BARN.

BARLEY! HEY! YOU HERE?

WHO'S THIS?

DON'T WORRY, BARLEY, THAT'S GRAYSTRIPE, MY OLD FRIEND FROM THUNDERCLAN.

AND SINCE YOU SAY YOU HAVE PLENTY...

...I'LL JUST TAKE ONE NOW.

THOSE ARE THUNDERCLAN HUNTING TECHNIQUES, AREN'T THEY?

SHE LEARNED QUICKLY.

I'M IMPRESSED. SHE'LL FIT IN WITH YOUR CLAN WELL, WON'T SHE?

IF WE CAN FIND THEM... YES, I EXPECT SHE WILL.

THERE'S A NIP IN THE AIR AS WE LEAVE THE NEXT MORNING.

NOBODY TALKS MUCH. BUT THERE'S A LOT THAT'S LEFT UNSAID. LOTS OF WORDS, LOTS OF FEELINGS.

RAVENPAW AND BARLEY ONLY AGREE TO GO WITH US UP TO HIGHSTONES.

AFTER THAT THEY'RE GOING BACK TO THEIR FARM...AND WE'RE ON OUR OWN.

STINKING TWOLEG TUNNELS LIKE THIS...

...STINKING TWOLEGS THEMSELVES...

HISSSSSS

NONE OF THIS IS FIT FOR A CLAN CAT. NOT FOR A WARRIOR.

I'VE GOT TO START DISTANCING MYSELF FROM ALL OF IT.

I DON'T EVEN STOP TO THINK FOR A SECOND THAT MILLIE MIGHT NOT FEEL THE SAME WAY.

I'M GETTING PRETTY HUNGRY. ARE YOU HUNGRY?

YEAH, I AM, NOW THAT YOU MENTION IT. COME ON, LET'S HUNT.

OH! HEY! THERE'S NO NEED!

HUH? WHAT DO YOU MEAN?

I BET THAT TWOLEG NEST WILL HAVE FOOD. IN FACT, I THINK I SEE A CAT FLAP IN THE BACK DOOR, SO WE CAN--

...BEGGING STARCLAN TO GUIDE THEM TO SAFETY.

IN THE BACK OF MY MIND I KNOW I'M GOING TO WAKE UP EXHAUSTED.

OH, THAT'S RIGHT. IT'S WRONG EVEN TO THINK ABOUT USING SOMETHING MADE BY TWOLEGS NOW, ISN'T IT?

THAT'S RIGHT.

WELL, I DIDN'T SEE YOU COMPLAINING TOO MUCH WHEN YOU LIVED WITH TWOLEGS.

YOU ATE THEIR FOOD. YOU LET THEM PET YOU.

AND I WAS WRONG TO DO THOSE THINGS.

I'M A WARRIOR. I NEED TO LIVE BY THE WARRIOR CODE.

SO LET'S STOP WASTING TIME AND GET ACROSS THIS FIELD.

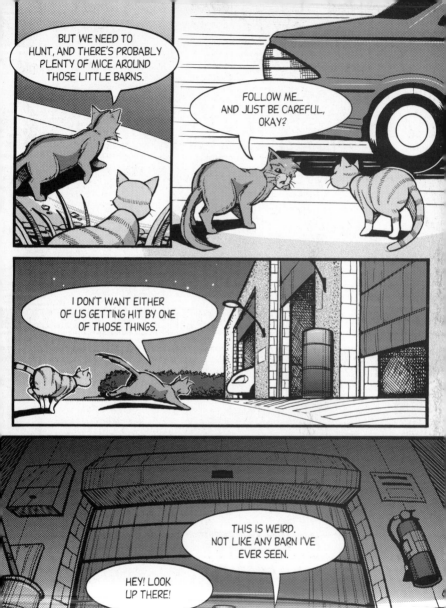

I DON'T KNOW IF IT'S BECAUSE I AM HUNGRY...OR IF I'M JUST TIRED OF ARGUING...BUT SUDDENLY I DON'T HAVE THE ENERGY.

OKAY. OKAY. YOU WIN. I'LL GO AND EAT.

HMM. WELL... THAT IS A LOT OF FOOD. JUST SITTING THERE, WAITING FOR ME...

PURRRRRRR...

YOU'RE NOT DIESEL!

YOU GET OUT OF HERE, YOU LOUSY STRAY!

GO ON! THAT'S NOT FOR YOU! GO ON, GET OUT!

RREEEEHHHRR!

LOOK, I DIDN'T KNOW THAT WAS GOING TO HAPPEN, I SWEAR. NOBODY BOTHERED ME WHEN I WAS IN THERE. I'M REALLY SORRY.

DID YOU... *AHEM.* DID YOU AT LEAST GET TO EAT ENOUGH?

DID I--

NO, I DIDN'T GET TO EAT ENOUGH! I BARELY HAD TWO BITES OF THAT REVOLTING GARBAGE YOU CALL FOOD!

I SHOULD'VE KNOWN! I SHOULD'VE KNOWN GOING INTO A TWOLEG PLACE WOULD BE A DISASTER!

AND YOU KNOW WHY I SHOULD'VE KNOWN? BECAUSE YOU SUGGESTED IT!

YOU'RE NO WARRIOR. YOU'RE STILL A KITTYPET! TWO-LEGS AND KITTYPET FOOD AND... AND *CAT FLAPS*...THEY'RE FOR YOU, NOT ME!

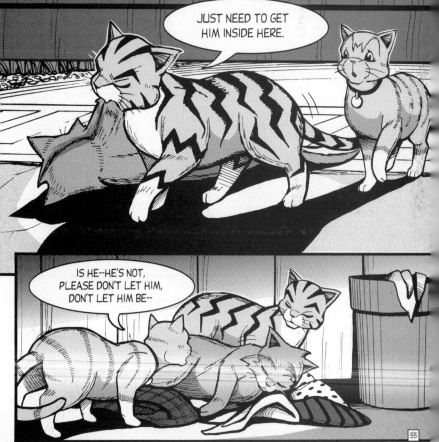

HE'S NOT DEAD, DON'T WORRY. I DON'T EVEN THINK HE'S THAT BADLY HURT.

THE TRUCK WASN'T GOING VERY FAST, AND IT JUST KNOCKED HIM BACKWARD.

I'VE SEEN OTHER CATS GET BACK UP FROM A LOT WORSE...

NAME'S DIESEL, BY THE WAY. WHAT'S YOURS?

HEY, WELCOME BACK, BRO.

I GOT BREAKFAST. MY TREAT.

THANKS.

THIS IS DIESEL, GRAYSTRIPE. HE LIVES HERE-- THIS PLACE IS CALLED A "TRUCKSTOP."

HE'S GOING TO LET US STAY HERE FOR A FEW DAYS, UNTIL YOU GET BETTER.

DID YOU ASK HIM IF HE'S SEEN THE CLAN CATS?

YEAH, SHE TOLD ME ALL ABOUT HOW YOU TWO ARE LOOKING FOR YOUR FRIENDS. SORRY, BRO, I HAVEN'T SEEN 'EM.

LOTS OF CATS PASSING THROUGH...EVERYBODY HERE'S JUST PASSING THROUGH...BUT NOBODY LIKE YOU'RE DESCRIBING.

I TOLD HIM WE WERE HEADING TOWARD THE SETTING SUN.

RIGHT. WHAT YOU'RE GONNA WANT TO DO IS TAKE THE ROAD. IT'LL POINT YOU STRAIGHT AT THE SEA.

THE "SEA"?
WHAT'S THAT?

I'VE NEVER BEEN MYSELF, BUT I'VE HEARD IT TALKED ABOUT.

IT'S LIKE THE BIGGEST STRETCH OF WATER YOU'VE EVER SEEN... AND THE SUN DROPS DOWN BEHIND IT EVERY NIGHT.

IN AN INSTANT I REALIZE HE'S TALKING ABOUT THE SUN-DROWN-PLACE.

THAT'S IT! THAT'S WHERE WE NEED TO GO.

THANKS FOR THE FOOD AND SHELTER, DIESEL, BUT WE'LL BE ON OUR WAY NOW.

HEY, NOW, GRAYSTRIPE, YOU'VE GOT HEART--AND LOTS OF IT, BRO, YOU'VE GOT MY RESPECT--

BUT YOU JUST GOT HIT BY A TRUCK.

tap

≶UFF≷

YOU'RE NOT GOIN' ANYWHERE. AT LEAST NOT FOR A WHILE.

BUT THEN I START TO REALIZE SOMETHING. I'VE BEEN THINKING IT ALL ALONG...

...BUT I DON'T THINK I'VE EVER ACTUALLY TOLD MILLIE HOW I FEEL ABOUT HER.

DIESEL'S RIGHT. I AM LUCKY.

BUT THEN--RIGHT WHEN I DECIDE TO TRY TO TELL HER--

AFTERNOON, FOLKS.

HEY, MILLIE, I TRIED THAT STALKING THING YOU SHOWED ME. IT WORKED GREAT. THANKS.

NO TROUBLE AT ALL, DIESEL. I'LL BE HAPPY TO TEACH YOU MORE IF YOU'D LIKE.

I'VE FELT LOST BEFORE... I'VE BEEN LOST BEFORE. BUT NEVER LIKE THIS.

NOW I FEEL LIKE I'M LOST, JUST SITTING HERE.

AFTER ALL THIS TIME, I'VE MADE UP MY MIND TO TALK TO MILLIE... REALLY TALK TO HER...

...AND EVERY CHANCE I GET, EITHER DIESEL'S THERE...

...OR SHE'S ACTING LIKE A MEDICINE CAT AND TELLING ME TO REST.

I'M NOT EVEN SURE HOW MANY DAYS GO BY LIKE THIS. I JUST KNOW I'M FRUSTRATED BEYOND WORDS.

HOW CAN YOU TELL?

IT SMELLS LIKE SALT AND FISH.

THAT ONE'S JUST COME FROM THE SEA.

THAT ONE'S FROM THE SEA, TOO.

THE YOUNG TWOLEGS USE THOSE BOARDS FOR SOME-THING. THEY GO TO THE SEA, AND THEIR SKIN'S ONE COLOR...

...THEN WHEN THEY COME BACK, THEY SMELL LIKE THE SEA, AND THEY'VE GOTTEN DARKER, AND THEY ALWAYS YELP A LOT.

AREN'T YOU EVER CURIOUS? DON'T YOU WANT TO SEE THIS PLACE YOURSELF?

NAH. I JUST DO MY OWN THING, Y'KNOW? AND MY THING IS HERE.

I BARELY PAY DIESEL ANY ATTENTION. I DON'T KNOW HOW HE CAN STAND LIVING HERE, SURROUNDED BY THE TWOLEGS AND THEIR MONSTERS.

MAC'S TRUCKSTOP

GAS

REPAIRS

RS

THUMP

HOW'S MY FAVORITE PATIENT?

I BROUGHT US A SNACK TO SHARE.

THANK YOU.

I REALLY APPRECIATE IT, BUT YOU KNOW, I CAN HUNT AGAIN. MY SHOULDER'S A LOT BETTER.

I KNOW.

I JUST LIKE DOING NICE THINGS FOR YOU.

THIS IS IT! THIS IS PERFECT. DEEP BREATHS...JUST SAY THE WORDS. *SAY THE WORDS.*

YES, ACTUALLY I--

MILLIE...DID YOU...DO YOU EVER WANT TO TELL SOMEONE SOME- THING, BUT YOU'RE NOT REALLY SURE HOW TO SAY IT?

BECAUSE I'VE BEEN--

OH, I'M SO SORRY! I JUST RAN RIGHT OVER YOU THERE.

OKAY, WELL... NOW, I KNOW YOU'RE GOING TO THINK THIS IS CRAZY. AND MAYBE IT IS A LITTLE BIT, BUT HEAR ME OUT.

ALL RIGHT...

NO, NO... YOU GO AHEAD.

WE COULD GET TO THE SEA BY RIDING ON ONE OF THE MONSTERS!

EXCUSE ME?

THE MONSTERS GO REALLY FAST, RIGHT? AND WE NEED TO GET TO THE SEA. AND YOUR SHOULDER'S STILL SORE, RIGHT?

SO EVEN IF WE WALKED, WE'D HAVE TO GO SLOW BECAUSE YOU'RE HURT, BUT IF WE RODE ON A MONSTER WE'D GET THERE IN NO TIME!

B-BUT, BUT THAT'S, IT'S, YOU'RE--YOU'RE OUT OF YOUR MIND, RIDING ON A MONSTER?

WHAT'RE YOU TALKING ABOUT?

I THINK IT COULD WORK.

I'VE BEEN THINKING ABOUT IT FOR A WHILE, AND I THINK IT'S A PRETTY GOOD IDEA.

IT TAKES ALL NIGHT FOR ME TO MAKE UP MY MIND. AND I'M STILL NOT CONVINCED IT'S THE RIGHT CHOICE.

BUT I THINK ABOUT MILLIE... AND FIRESTAR... AND I KNOW IT'S A CHOICE I HAVE TO MAKE.

NAH, THAT ONE'S NO GOOD. IT'S BEEN THERE, BUT IT'S HEADING AWAY FROM THE SEA NOW.

AND THE LITTLE ONE, THERE'S NOWHERE TO HOLD ON. THE TWOLEGS WOULD SEE YOU.

SO WHAT ARE WE LOOKING FOR?

AHA!

YOU'RE LOOKING FOR THAT.

IT'S GOT THE BOARDS. IT'S HEADED TOWARD THE SEA. AND YOU CAN HIDE IN THE BACK PART WITHOUT EVER BEING SEEN.

A PERFECT CHOICE, IF I DO SAY SO MYSELF.

THANK YOU, DIESEL. YOU'VE BEEN FANTASTIC TO US.

YEAH. THANK YOU.

YOU COULD ALWAYS COME WITH US, YOU KNOW.

NAH, I BELONG HERE. MEANT TO BE A LONER.

BESIDES, I MEET TOO MANY INTERESTING CATS TO GIVE THIS UP.

HURRY NOW, OR THE MONSTERS WILL LEAVE YOU BEHIND.

I CAN'T BELIEVE I'M DOING THIS...

GOOD-BYE!

I REALLY CAN'T BELIEVE I'M DOING THIS...!

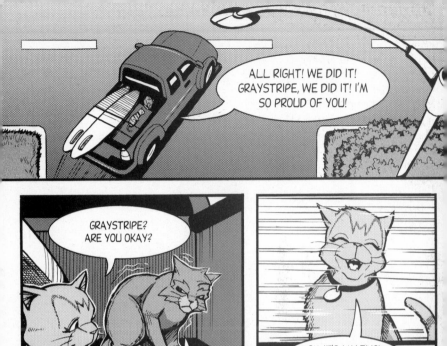

ALL RIGHT! WE DID IT! GRAYSTRIPE, WE DID IT! I'M SO PROUD OF YOU!

GRAYSTRIPE? ARE YOU OKAY?

I'M FINE...

...JUST BASKING IN ALL THE PRIDE...

OH, IT'S AMAZING! HAVE YOU EVER FELT THE WIND IN YOUR FUR LIKE THIS?

IT'S LIKE RUNNING FASTER THAN I'VE EVER RUN BEFORE!

WHEEEEEE!

IT FEELS LIKE WE'RE SLOWING DOWN.

ARE WE THERE?

OH... NO, THIS CAN'T BE IT. I DON'T SEE ANY WATER ANYWHERE.

HARE HILL INN

I GUESS THE TWO-LEGS ARE STOPPING FOR THE NIGHT.

BETTER GET OUT BEFORE THEY SEE US. LET'S TRY TO HUNT.

WHEREVER WE ARE, I HATE IT. THE BEST WE CAN DO IS A FILTHY RAT, AND THE WATER OUT OF A MUD PUDDLE.

THE WHOLE PLACE SMELLS LIKE CROW-FOOD. I'M AMAZED MILLIE CAN SLEEP.

I STILL WANT TO TALK TO HER... I NEED TO. BUT NOT HERE.

NOT YET.

BESIDES, I CAN'T SHAKE THE FEELING THAT WE'RE BEING WATCHED.

GRAYSTRIPE?

WHAT'S WRONG?

KITTYPETS. I CAN TELL BY THEIR SCENT ALONE. WE'RE BEING ATTACKED BY KITTYPETS. AT FIRST I'M MORE ANNOYED THAN ANYTHING...

KLANG

...BUT I REALIZE THESE AREN'T PAMPERED WEAKLINGS. THESE ARE MORE LIKE DUKE. I GET READY TO FIGHT, AND FIGHT HARD. BUT THEN...

I CAN BARELY TALK ONCE I GET BACK ONTO THE MONSTER WITH MILLIE.

NOW MY PAW AND MY SHOULDER HURT SO MUCH I'M TOO DISTRACTED TO TALK.

OR...WELL...THAT MIGHT JUST BE AN EXCUSE...

WHY CAN'T I TELL MILLIE HOW I FEEL? WHY IS THIS SO HARD?

GRAYSTRIPE! GRAYSTRIPE!

HUH? WHAT?

LOOK!

WHAT? WHAT DO YOU SEE?

AND IF FIRESTAR IS LEADING THEM, THEY WOULDN'T GO SOMEWHERE THAT HAD NO TREES.

THEY WOULDN'T SETTLE IN A TWOLEG-PLACE.

BUT THERE...

COME ON. IT'S THAT WAY. NOW THAT WE'RE HERE...

...I CAN ALMOST FEEL IT.

EVERYTHING'S SO QUIET AS WE ENTER THE FOREST. NO TWOLEGS... NO MONSTERS.

BUT THE QUIET DOESN'T LAST FOR LONG.

DID YOU HEAR THAT?

YEAH.

FOLLOW ME.

THE MOU--?

NO, NO, NO, LISTEN, WE DON'T WANT THE MOUSE. THE MOUSE IS YOURS.

UH... OKAY THEN... WHAT DO YOU WANT?

HAVE YOU SEEN A LARGE GROUP OF CATS COME THROUGH HERE?

LARGE...UH... LARGE GROUP...LET ME THINK...

OH, WAIT--YEAH! YEAH, THERE'S A BIG GROUP OVER THIS RIDGE... BUT I WOULDN'T GO OVER THERE IF I WERE YOU.

I'VE HEARD THEY EAT BONES!

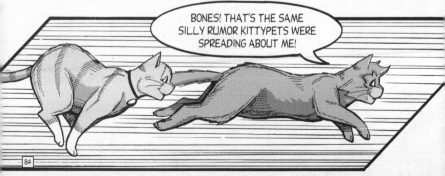

BONES! THAT'S THE SAME SILLY RUMOR KITTYPETS WERE SPREADING ABOUT ME!

...IT'D BE TIME FOR THE GATHERING NOW.

THAT WOULD...THAT WOULD MAKE SENSE...

WOW...IT'S BEAUTIFUL...

ARE YOU READY? SHOULD WE GO DOWN?

ACTUALLY...MILLIE... I WANT TO TALK WITH YOU FIRST.

YEAH?

UH-OH...THIS LOOKS SERIOUS.

I'VE BEEN TRYING TO FIGURE OUT HOW TO SAY THIS...OR WHEN TO SAY THIS... FOR DAYS NOW.

MILLIE, I...I KNOW I'VE BEEN HARD TO DEAL WITH. AND I KNOW THIS LIFE CAN BE HARD.

WARRIORS

THE RISE OF SCOURGE

WARRIORS

CATS of the CLANS

ERIN HUNTER

ILLUSTRATED BY WAYNE McLOUGHLIN

MEET THE CLANS' HEROES IN

WARRIORS
CATS of the CLANS

Hear the stories of the great warriors as they've never been told before! Chock-full of visual treats and captivating details, including full-color illustrations and in-depth biographies of important cats from all four Clans, from fierce Clan leaders to wise medicine cats to the most mischievous kits.

WARRIORS

FIELD GUIDE

SECRETS
OF THE
CLANS

ERIN HUNTER
ILLUSTRATED BY WAYNE McLOUGHLIN

GO DEEP INSIDE THE CLANS WITH

WARRIORS

FIELD GUIDE

SECRETS
OF THE
CLANS

Explore the warrior Clan camps with an insiders-only tour guided by a warrior cat. Find out the secrets of how an apprentice learns to fight, hunt, and live by the warrior code. Understand the lore of healing herbs passed down from one medicine cat to another. Discover the never-before-revealed myths, legends, and mystical origins of the warrior Clans.

WARRIORS

SUPER EDITION

FIRESTAR'S QUEST

An all-new adventure for ThunderClan's hero

ERIN HUNTER

JOIN THUNDERCLAN'S LEADER FIRESTAR ON
HIS GREATEST ADVENTURE EVER IN

FIRESTAR'S QUEST

There is peace at last between the warrior Clans and
all four are thriving, training new warriors, and keeping
their boundaries without conflict. Then Firestar,
legendary leader of ThunderClan, discovers a shocking
secret: StarClan, the warrior ancestors who guide his
paw steps, have lied to him.

Firestar must embark on a perilous quest to discover a
truth that has been buried beyond the memory of living
cats. Whatever he finds at the end of his journey, he's
sure of one thing: Nothing can ever be the same again.

SEEKERS

THE QUEST BEGINS

ERIN HUNTER

SEEKERS

THE QUEST BEGINS

TURN THE PAGE FOR A
PEEK AT THE FIRST BOOK IN
ERIN HUNTER'S BRAND-NEW
SERIES, SEEKERS.

When three young bears from different species—black, polar, and grizzly—are separated from their families, they each face great dangers and terrible tragedies, and situations that will require all their strength to survive.

CHAPTER ONE

Kallik

"A *long, long time ago, long* before bears walked the earth, a frozen sea shattered into pieces, scattering tiny bits of ice across the darkness of the sky. Each of those pieces of ice contains the spirit of a bear, and if you are good, and brave, and strong, one day your spirit will join them."

Kallik leaned against her mother's hind leg, listening to the story she had heard so many times before. Beside her, her brother, Taqqiq, stretched, batting at the snowy walls of the den with his paws. He was always restless when the weather trapped them inside.

"When you look carefully at the sky," Kallik's mother continued, "you can see a pattern of stars in the shape of the Great Bear, Silaluk. She is running around and around the Pathway Star."

"Why is she running?" Kallik chipped in. She knew the answer, but this was the part of the story where she always asked.

"Because it is snow-sky and she is hunting. With her quick and powerful claws, she hunts seal and beluga whale. She is the greatest of all hunters on the ice."

Kallik loved hearing about Silaluk's strength.

"But then the ice melts," Nisa said in a hushed voice. "And she can't hunt anymore. She gets hungrier and hungrier, but she has to keep running because three hunters pursue her: Robin, Chickadee, and Moose Bird. They chase her for many moons, all through the warm days, until the end of burn-sky. Then, as the warmth begins to leave the earth, they finally catch up to her.

"They gather around her and strike the fatal blow with their spears. The heart's blood of the Great Bear falls to the ground, and everywhere it falls the leaves on the trees turn red and yellow. Some of the blood falls on Robin's chest, and that is why the bird has a red breast."

"Does the Great Bear die?" breathed Taqqiq.

"She does," Nisa replied. Kallik shivered. Every time she heard this story it frightened her all over again. Her mother went on.

"But then snow-sky returns, bringing back the ice. Silaluk is reborn and the ice-hunt begins all over again, season after season."

Kallik snuggled into her mother's soft white fur. The walls of the den curved up and around them, making a sheltering cave of snow that Kallik could barely glimpse in the dark, although it was only a few pawlengths from her nose. Outside a fierce wind howled across the ice, sending tendrils of freezing air through the entrance tunnel into their den. Kallik was glad they didn't have to be out there tonight.

Inside the den, she and her brother were warm and safe. Kallik wondered if Silaluk had ever had a mother and brother, or a den where she could hide from the storms. If the Great Bear had a family to keep her safe, maybe she wouldn't have to run from the hunters. Kallik knew her mother would protect her from anything scary until she was big enough and strong enough and smart enough to protect herself.

Taqqiq batted at Kallik's nose with his large furry paw. "Kallik's scared," he teased. She could make out his eyes gleaming in the darkness.

"Am not!" Kallik protested.

"She thinks robins and chickadees are going to come after her," Taqqiq said with an amused rumble.

"No, I don't!" Kallik growled, digging her claws into the snow. "That's not why I'm scared!"

"Ha! You *are* scared! I knew it!"

Nisa nudged Kallik gently with her muzzle. "Why are you frightened, little one? You've heard the legend of the Great Bear many times before."

"I know," Kallik said. "It's just . . . it reminds me that soon snow-sky will be over, and the snow and ice will all melt away. And then we won't be able to hunt anymore, and we'll be hungry all the time. Right? Isn't that what happens during burn-sky?"

Kallik's mother sighed, her massive shoulders shifting under her snow-white pelt. "Oh, my little star," she murmured. "I didn't mean to worry you." She touched her black nose to Kallik's. "You haven't lived through a burn-sky yet, Kallik. It's not as terrible as it sounds. We'll find a way to survive, even if it means eating berries and grass for a little while."

"What is berries and grass?" Kallik asked.

Taqqiq wrinkled his muzzle. "Does it taste as good as seals?"

"No," Nisa said, "but berries and grass will keep you alive, which is the important thing. I'll show them to you when we reach land." She fell silent. For a few heartbeats, all Kallik could hear was the thin wail of the wind battering at the snowy walls.

She pressed closer to her mother, feeling the warmth radiating from her skin. "Are you sad?" she whispered.

Nisa touched Kallik with her muzzle again. "Don't be afraid," she said, a note of determination in her voice. "Remember the story of the Great Bear. No matter what happens, the ice will always return. And all the bears gather on the edge of the sea to meet it. Silaluk will always get back on her paws. She's a survivor, and so are we."